A LITTLE PRINCESS

A LITTLE PRINCESS

FRANCES HODGSON BURNETT

Retold by
Carol Adorjan

Illustrated by
Frederic Marvin

Troll Associates

Library of Congress Cataloging in Publication Data

Adorjan, Carol Madden.
   A little princess.

   Summary: When she is orphaned, the star pupil of
Miss Minchin's boarding school in London becomes a
penniless, friendless ward of the cruel Miss Minchin.
   [1. Boarding schools—Fiction.   2. Schools—Fiction.
3. Orphans—Fiction.   4. London (England)—Fiction]
I. Marvin, Frederic, ill.   II. Burnett, Frances
Hodgson, 1849-1924.   Little princess.   III. Title.
PZ7.A2618Li   1988   [Fic]   87-15485
ISBN 0-8167-1201-8 (lib. bdg.)
ISBN 0-8167-1202-6 (pbk.)

Sara Crewe stood close beside her father at the bottom of a flight of stairs leading up to a tall, narrow house. A brass sign on the door read: Miss Minchin's School for Girls.

Sara hugged Emily, the new doll her father had bought her. Sara's large, blue eyes were sad. "Is this the place?" she asked.

Captain Crewe looked down at his daughter. "Yes," he answered. "This is where you'll be staying."

Sara slipped her hand into his. Just as they were about to go up the stairs, they heard loud shouts behind them. Out of the London fog came several children, all laughing, talking, and looking very much alike. One big happy family, Sara thought, feeling even sadder.

As the children passed by, Captain Crewe said, "You see how happy everyone is, Sara? London is a good place to live. Before long, you'll be right at home here."

Sara wasn't so sure. Up until now she had lived her whole life in India, where her father would now return. No place would seem like home without him.

Captain Crewe squeezed her hand as they went up the stairs. Sara's mother had died when she was born, so Sara and her father were especially close. He knew what she was thinking. He knew Sara would be lonely without him, just as he would be lonely without her.

"It's for the best," he told her. "You'll meet girls your own age and learn lots of new things. Every day will be a new adventure."

Sara brightened. "And before long, we'll have a vacation," she said. "Then you'll come to get Emily and me."

Captain Crewe laughed as he opened the heavy door for Sara. "That's my brave little soldier," he said.

Inside, a tall, thin woman emerged from the shadows.

"Ah, Captain Crewe," she said. "We've been expecting you." She turned her large, fishlike eyes on Sara.

"This must be Sara. What a beautiful child!"

Sara felt uncomfortable. She didn't
think of herself as beautiful, and she didn't
believe the woman really meant what she said.
"How do you do, Miss Minchin," she said politely.

"Your rooms are ready," Miss Minchin said. Then she
smiled at Captain Crewe. The smile didn't seem to fit her
face, and Sara was sure the woman was not in the habit of
smiling. "We hope Sara will be comfortable here."

"Has Mariette arrived?" Captain Crewe asked. Mariette
was a French maid he had hired for Sara.

"She is expected any minute," Miss Minchin replied.

All along the hall, doors opened a crack as they walked
by. Children peeked out, eager to see this new girl whose
father was rich and who had come from a far-off place.

Lotte Legh, the youngest girl, thought Sara looked
elegant. "See her clothes!" she murmured to the others.
"And oh, that beautiful doll! They're even dressed alike!"

"She looks like a princess," one of the other girls said.

The oldest girl, Lavinia, frowned. Until now, she had been
thought of as the girls' leader. She didn't like the idea that
someone else might take her place.

Upstairs, Miss Minchin opened the door on a light, airy room filled with Sara's own things from home. Sara's clothes trunk, which had arrived just before she did, stood in the center of the room. A smaller suitcase was beside it.

A girl about Sara's age knelt by the fireplace. Soot smudges lined her face and coal dust clung to her ragged black dress.

Sara didn't seem to notice the girl's appearance. "Hello, I'm Sara Crewe," she said. "What's your name?"

Standing behind Sara, her hands on her hips, Miss Minchin gave the ragged girl a disapproving look.

Without a word, the girl grabbed her coal bucket and moved quickly out of the room.

Sara was puzzled. "Who was that?" she asked. "And why did she go away like that?"

Miss Minchin waved away Sara's concern. "That was Becky," she said. "She should have had that fire going hours ago. She left because she knows servants have no business talking to my girls."

Sara didn't understand that. Servants were surely the same as everyone else. Only their jobs were different.

Her father motioned her to the front window. "Look here," he said. "You have a fine view of the whole street."

Outside, the children they had seen when they arrived were playing noisily. The "Large Family" is what Sara decided to call them. "Do they live nearby?" she asked Miss Minchin.

"Down the street," Miss Minchin answered. "A very noisy brood. Their father is a lawyer. You'd think he'd be stricter with them."

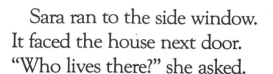

Sara ran to the side window. It faced the house next door. "Who lives there?" she asked.

"No one," Miss Minchin told her. "That house is empty. Has been for years."

Somehow, this news made Sara sad.

"If you need anything," added Miss Minchin, "just call." She then excused herself and left the room.

When they were alone, Captain Crewe put his arm around Sara. "Well, my little princess, what do you think?"

"It's a lovely room," Sara said. But she suddenly felt like crying. Her father would leave soon and she would be alone.

"I'll miss you, Sara," her father said.

Sara threw her arms around him. I won't cry, she thought. I'll be a brave soldier. "I'll miss you too, Papa."

He looked at her long and hard. "You'll be all right," he said. It sounded more like a question.

"I have Emily," Sara said, holding the doll close.

Captain Crewe smiled. "You made the right choice. She'll be good company."

Emily was a beautiful doll with curly golden-brown hair and deep, clear-blue eyes. Captain Crewe thought the doll had an intelligent expression. He and Sara had shopped all over London and had nearly given up hope of finding just the right doll until Sara saw her in a shop window. It was as though Emily had been waiting for them.

Captain Crewe gave his daughter one last hug and then he left the room. Sara ran to the front window, waving to her father as he climbed into the waiting carriage and drove away. She leaned out the window a little to watch until the horse and carriage disappeared around the corner. It was then that Sara took a closer look at the empty house beside the school. Its windows stared at her blankly.

"I'm as empty as that house," Sara told Emily.

There was a knock at the door and Mariette, the French maid, peeked in. "Is someone here with you, Sara?" she asked.

Sara was happy to see her. "Just Emily," she said, showing her the doll. "We were talking."

As they unpacked Sara's trunk, Sara told Mariette what she believed about dolls. "They can do things they won't let us know about," she explained. "Emily can probably read and talk and walk, but she'll only do it when no one's around. Because if people knew dolls could do all that, they'd make them work. It's a secret. Someday, though, Emily might trust me enough to let me catch her at it."

Mariette's laugh was warm and comforting. It made Sara feel less lonely.

11

The next morning, when Sara entered the classroom, everyone stared wide-eyed at her. Sara sat quietly at her desk and looked back at them. She wondered if they liked the school and if any of them had a papa like hers.

Miss Minchin rapped on her desk for attention. "Sara," she said, "since your father hired a French maid, I assume he wants you to study French."

Sara stood up. She didn't know what to say. "I think he hired her because I . . . like her," she said.

Miss Minchin's mouth tightened into a narrow line. "You are a spoiled child," she said, "thinking everything is done just because you like it that way. Your father must want you to learn French."

Sara couldn't remember a time when she didn't know French! It had always been spoken to her. Her mother had been French, and her father loved the language. But now she was embarrassed and didn't know how to explain. "I . . . I have never . . . really . . . *learned* French," she began shyly.

Her classmates snickered.

"Enough," Miss Minchin interrupted. "You will begin lessons just as soon as Mr. Dufarge gets here. Until then, look at this book."

Sara's cheeks felt warm. She took the book to her desk.

When Mr. Dufarge entered the room, he smiled at Sara. "Is this a new pupil for me?" he asked.

"Her father wants her to learn French," declared Miss Minchin, "but *she* doesn't want to!"

Sara stood up slowly. She had to do something to make them understand. In French, she explained that Miss Minchin had not understood. She had not learned French in a schoolroom—she had always *known* it.

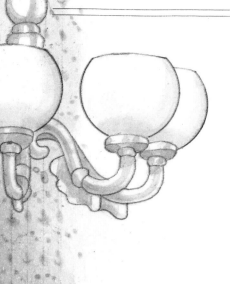

Mr. Dufarge smiled. "Miss Minchin," he said, "I can't teach French to Sara. She *is* French. She could be my helper."

Miss Minchin was embarrassed and angry. She turned on Sara. "You should have *told* me!" she scolded.

"I...I tried," Sara said.

The other girls giggled behind their books.

Miss Minchin's face turned red. "Silence!" she demanded.

During the regular French class that followed, Sara noticed a girl with fair hair tightly braided. She was pronouncing words incorrectly and had trouble remembering. Some of the others laughed at her.

Sara went over to her after class. "My name's Sara Crewe," she said. "What's yours?"

The girl could not believe that this princess from a faraway land had come over just to talk to her. "Er—Ermengarde Saint-John," she stammered.

"Would you like to see Emily?" Sara asked.

"Who's Emily?"

"Come see," Sara said. She led Ermengarde upstairs. "We must be very quiet, or we won't catch her."

Ermengarde was puzzled, but she asked no questions. Instead, feeling pleased and excited about being included, she followed along on tiptoe.

At the door to her room, Sara paused and took a deep breath. Then she suddenly threw the door wide open.

Inside, the loveliest doll Ermengarde had ever seen sat in a chair with a book in its lap.

"Oh," Sara said, disappointment in her voice. "She knew we were coming. She got back in her chair."

Ready to believe anything, Ermengarde said, "She can...walk?"

"Of course," Sara said."All dolls walk."

Ermengarde's eyes grew large. Dolls were nice to have and hold, but she had never thought about them *doing* anything.

"I've never actually *seen* her," Sara explained, "but I think she can. I *pretend* she can. Don't you ever pretend things?"

Ermengarde shook her head. "Like what?" she asked.

"All sorts of things," Sara said. Then she told Ermengarde about her home in India and how she could pretend she was back there in her own room. She told her new friend about the "Large Family" down the block. "I pretend I know them, you see. I've even given them a name. I call them the Montmorencys. I got that name from a book."

Ermengarde was delighted. She had never met anyone as interesting as Sara.

"It makes things easier...pretending," Sara said. Her eyes grew sad. She was thinking about her papa. "Do you love your father more than anything in the whole world?" she asked.

Ermengarde didn't know what to say. She didn't know her own father very well. "I don't see much of him," she replied.

"That's too bad," Sara said. "But you could *pretend* you did. I pretend Papa's away for the day, and at night I fall asleep waiting for him to come home and kiss me good night."

After a long silence, Ermengarde said, "I wish we could be best friends."

Sara's eyes lit up. She smiled. "I'd like that. And I will help you with your French."

One day, as Sara was passing the sitting room, she heard Lotte Legh, the youngest girl, crying. Miss Minchin and her sister, Miss Amelia, were trying to quiet Lotte. They pleaded and scolded, but nothing worked. Lotte cried harder. Finally, Miss Minchin threw up her hands without hope.

"Maybe I could help," Sara offered.

Miss Minchin was happy to let her try.

When she was alone with Lotte, Sara sat down on the floor beside her. Lotte's eyes were closed tightly and she kept

wailing. Sara said nothing. Finally, Lotte opened her eyes.

"I haven't got a mama," she howled.

"Neither have I," Sara said.

Suddenly, Lotte stopped crying. Sara didn't have a mother either! Then she must know what it was like to feel alone. Lotte wiped her eyes. She felt very close to Sara.

Sara stayed with her, telling her stories, until Lotte was able to smile and return to her classroom.

Sara was like that: helpful and kind. Before long, all the girls—except Lavinia—loved her as Ermengarde and Lotte did. And Sara was such a wonderful storyteller that everyone gathered around her during their free time to listen to her stories.

A few evenings later, when Sara was telling a story about a princess, Becky came into the sitting room to add coals to the fire. Sara's story was so interesting that the girl forgot her work and listened. At an especially exciting part in the story, she dropped the fireplace shovel.

Lavinia looked around. "That girl has been listening!" she cried angrily.

Becky leaped to her feet and scurried from the room.

"I knew she was listening," Sara said quietly. "Why shouldn't she?"

"My mother wouldn't let me tell stories to servant girls," Lavinia snapped.

"Stories belong to everyone," Sara told her.

Later, in her room, Sara found Becky asleep in an easy chair near the bright, crackling fire.

Becky awoke with a frightened gasp. "Oh, Miss Sara," she said as she struggled to her feet. "I'm sorry. I...I..."

Becky looked tired and hungry, and Sara felt sorry that she had to work so hard. After all, she was only a little girl like herself. Then she remembered the cake she'd saved.

"I'm glad you're here," Sara said. "We can have a party." She gave Becky the thick slice of cake, talking and asking questions to make Becky feel at ease.

"Do you like stories?" Sara asked.

Becky could only nod.

"If you tell me what time you come to my room, I'll try to be here. I'll tell you a bit of a story every day until it's finished. And then, I'll start a new one!"

Becky left the room as happy as she could be. She had an extra piece of cake in her pocket and she was warm. Most important of all, she had a good friend in Sara.

19

Friendship was also important to Sara. Sharing made her life brighter—as did letters from her father. In one of his letters he wrote that he and an old friend had become partners. Diamonds had been found on his friend's land, and the two of them were going to mine them.

"Diamond mines," Sara said to her friends. "Just imagine!" In her mind she could see the dark mine passages and the sparkling stones in the walls and ceilings. She could see men with picks digging out the diamonds. She made up wonderful stories about it all. Everyone seemed to be interested in Captain Crewe's diamond mines.

Certainly Miss Minchin was. Captain Crewe, already rich, could now bring in even more money to the school. She was especially nice to Sara.

"Your eleventh birthday will come soon," she announced one day. "We'll arrange a wonderful celebration."

By the time that day arrived, the whole school was in a whirl of excitement. Sara, in her best silk dress, led the other girls into the classroom. Everyone oohed and aahed at the colorful decorations. Then Becky and some of the other servants brought in wrapped box after wrapped box.

Miss Minchin gave a speech, saying Sara was a lovely girl and surely deserved this special birthday party.

Sara listened, knowing Miss Minchin didn't mean what she said. Though she was glad to see everyone enjoying the party, Sara missed her father more than ever.

The children crowded around Sara, clamoring for her to open her presents. She had just begun to do so when Miss Minchin was called away.

A sharp-featured man waited for Miss Minchin in her office. He was Mr. Barrow, Captain Crewe's lawyer.

Miss Minchin thought he was bringing her money. It had been a long time since she had received a check from Captain Crewe. "Are the diamond mines going well?" she asked Mr. Barrow eagerly.

"Diamond mines! Ha!" he said. "Diamond mines spell ruin more often than wealth."

Miss Minchin felt faint. "Do you mean to say Captain Crewe has lost his money?"

"And his life," Mr. Barrow added sadly. "Fever and business troubles."

The words struck Miss Minchin like a blow. Not for a moment did she think about Sara and how sad the child would be. She thought only of herself. "Do you mean to tell me that Sara is now but a beggar on my hands?"

Mr. Barrow nodded. "Her father left her nothing. And as far as we know, she has no relatives."

Miss Minchin steadied herself against her desk. "I've been cheated! I've paid all her bills since the last check came! I'll—I'll turn her out on the street, that's what I'll do!"

"I wouldn't do that," Mr. Barrow cautioned. "If people heard about it, they might not send their girls to your school. Keep her here. When she's older, she can work for you."

Miss Minchin went white with rage. "When she's *older*? Hah! She'll work for me *now*!"

When Mr. Barrow left, Miss Minchin sent for Miss Amelia. She told her what had happened. "Tell Sara to find a black dress to put on. Then bring her here. 'The Little Princess' has just lost her crown."

When Sara came into Miss Minchin's office, she was not the happy butterfly-child of the party. The black dress she wore was an old velvet one, too short and too tight. Because she couldn't find a black ribbon, her thick black hair tumbled loosely around her pale, stricken face.

"I suppose Miss Amelia told you what has happened," Miss Minchin said curtly.

"Yes," Sara answered. "My papa is ... dead."

Miss Minchin's temper rose. "And you are a beggar! I have already sent Mariette away. Now you are alone in the world."

Sara looked the woman in the eye. Although she felt as though her heart had been broken, she didn't cry. And that made Miss Minchin angrier!

"Don't put on grand airs with me," the woman said. "You are *not* a princess. You're like Becky. You'll run errands and help in the kitchen and schoolroom. If you don't do as I say, I'll send you away. Now go!"

Sara turned to leave.

"Stop!" Miss Minchin commanded. "Aren't you even going to thank me?"

"What for?" said Sara, and then she ran from the room.

Upstairs, Miss Amelia was standing at the door to her room. "This is not your room anymore," she said.

"Where is my room?" Sara asked. She hoped her voice didn't shake.

"In the attic, next to Becky's," Miss Amelia told her.

Her new room was dirty, damp, and bare. There was a rusty iron coal stove, a hard bed covered with an old, faded cover, and a wooden table. The only window was high up near the ceiling.

Sara sat on the edge of the bed. She fought back the tears. "I'll be a good soldier, Papa," she said. Then she fell back across the bed. "My papa is dead!" she whispered to herself. "My papa is dead!" All through the long night she called to him.

Early the next morning, Sara was put to work. She helped clean up the school's breakfast dishes and swept the floor. She taught the younger children French and helped with their other lessons. Then, after school, she returned to the kitchen where she helped prepare dinner and clean up. It was a long day.

Finally, Sara was allowed to return to her attic room. There she tried to get out of her dress. But the buttons were in the back, and her arms were so tired that she couldn't reach. She was still struggling with the dress when there was a knock at the door.

Becky slipped in. "I brought you some coal," she said. She began to light a fire and then helped Sara off with her dress. "Remember, I'm close by—just on the other side of this wall," she told Sara.

Dear Becky, thought Sara. She's every bit as tired as I am, and yet she wants to help in every way.

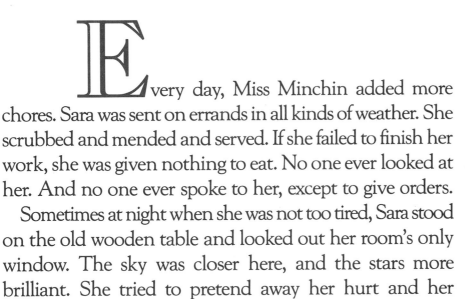

Every day, Miss Minchin added more chores. Sara was sent on errands in all kinds of weather. She scrubbed and mended and served. If she failed to finish her work, she was given nothing to eat. No one ever looked at her. And no one ever spoke to her, except to give orders.

Sometimes at night when she was not too tired, Sara stood on the old wooden table and looked out her room's only window. The sky was closer here, and the stars more brilliant. She tried to pretend away her hurt and her loneliness, but all she could do was stare at the empty attic window next door. Sara's heart ached. She could not pretend it didn't. She never told anyone how she felt. Whom could she tell? Even Emily, her precious doll, had been taken from her. It was just as well. There was nothing to say. Sara's grief had dried up the well of words.

"Soldiers don't complain," she would mutter between her clenched teeth.

She repeated that to herself one day as she carried the mending downstairs. She didn't notice Ermengarde in the hall below.

Ermengarde had been called home right after Sara's party and had just returned to the school. The other girls had told her what had happened, but she wasn't prepared to see Sara looking so pale and strange in her outgrown dress.

"Sara?" she said. "Is that you?"

Sara didn't answer. She's just like the others, she thought. She doesn't really want to talk to me.

"How are you?" Ermengarde asked.

"I don't know, " Sara replied. "How are you?"

The coldness in Sara's voice made Ermengarde shy and uneasy. "Are you very . . . unhappy?"

The ache in Sara's heart swelled. How could anyone be so stupid? she wondered. "What do you think?" she snapped. "Do you think I'm very happy?" And she marched past Ermengarde without another word.

For several weeks after that, Sara looked the other way whenever they met. Ermengarde was confused and hurt. She was so unhappy that she couldn't join in the others' games. She sat alone thinking about her best friend, Sara.

One night, when Sara climbed up to her attic room, she found someone sitting on her battered footstool and wearing a red shawl.

"Ermengarde!" she said. "You shouldn't be here. You'll get in trouble."

Ermengarde's eyes and nose were pink with crying. "I don't care," she said. "Oh, Sara, please tell me why you don't like me anymore."

Sara felt a lump in her throat. "I *do* like you," she said. "It's just that everything's . . . changed. You're . . . different."

"You're the one who's different," Ermengarde said. "You didn't want to talk to me and . . ."

"I thought you didn't want to talk to *me*! No one else does," Sara said.

"Oh, Sara!" Ermengarde wailed.

Then they rushed into each other's arms and hugged like the good friends they were.

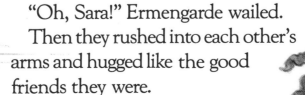

Lotte was more puzzled than anyone with the changes in her beloved Sara. She could not understand why Sara always wore the same black dress or why someone else lived in Sara's old room. She asked, but Sara didn't answer. Sara was afraid Miss Minchin might hear and be angry with Lotte for talking to Sara. But Lotte was determined to find the answers to her questions.

Late one afternoon, Lotte had seen Sara go up the attic stairs. Lotte followed her. She found Sara standing on the table and looking out the window. Lotte looked around at the ugly, bare room. It made her sad to think her beautiful Sara lived here.

"Sara!" she said, her voice tearful.

Sara turned at the sound of her voice. She knew that if Lotte cried, she would too. "Don't cry," she said quickly. "It's not such a bad room, Lotte. You can see all sorts of things from here you can't see downstairs."

Lotte climbed up on the table beside Sara.

"See all the chimneys?" Sara said. "Look at the smoke curling up in wreaths."

"And clouds!" Lotte said. "And all those birds!"

Lotte took a bun from her pocket. They crumbled it and fed the sparrows.

"It's really a lovely room," Sara said. "In the morning, I can watch the sunrise, and at night, the sunset."

"Oh, Sara," Lotte said, "I want to live here too!"

When Lotte went downstairs again, the happiness of the moment went with her. Sara stayed at the window, looking out. The window across the way stared blankly at her. "If only someone lived there," she said softly to herself. "Sometimes this is the loneliest place in the world." But in

the attic, at least, she could talk to Ermengarde and Lotte when they sneaked upstairs to see her. They couldn't do that often, for fear of being caught. But it was better than nothing. And she had Becky. Usually both of them were too tired at the end of the day to talk much, but it was good to know there was a friend on the other side of the wall.

Even if she had lost most of her friends in school, once outside, Sara still had the "Large Family." She looked for them eagerly when she ran errands. There were eight children, she learned, and their real name was Carmichael.

One evening at Christmas time, when Sara was returning to Miss Minchin's, the Carmichael children were climbing into their carriage. They were dressed in party clothes. Sara forgot her basket and her shabby cape and stopped to watch.

The smallest boy saw Sara standing in the shadows, cold and hungry. He had heard Christmas stories about kind people giving poor children money. He had a coin in his pocket, so he took it out and offered it to her.

"Here, poor little girl," he said.

Sara's face went red. "Oh, no!" she said. "I couldn't take your money."

She didn't sound like a street child. The boy's older sisters, Janet and Nora, leaned forward to listen.

The little boy said, "I want you to have it."

His face was so honest and kind, Sara knew she'd hurt his feelings if she refused. She took the coin. "Thank you," she said. "You are a kind, little darling."

A beggar would never say a thing like that, thought Janet and Nora.

From that time on, the "Large Family" was as interested in Sara as she was in it. Faces appeared at bedroom windows when Sara passed. They talked about her often, calling her the-little-girl-who-is-not-a-beggar.

No matter how hungry she got, Sara never spent the coin. She wore it on a faded ribbon around her neck.

One day, Sara saw a large wagon full of furniture next door. The house would no longer be empty! She was excited and curious. Who would live in the empty house? Would someone take the attic room?

That night, Becky brought her news.

"It's an Indian gentleman who's coming to live next door," she said. "He's very rich, but he's had lots of trouble and he's sick. The father of the ' Large Family ' is his lawyer."

An Indian gentleman, Sara thought. Someone from home!

Several days later, Sara was returning from an errand when a carriage pulled up to the house. Mr. Carmichael got out first. A nurse and a servant followed. They helped their employer, a thin, sick man wrapped in furs. Sara's heart went out to him because he looked so unhappy.

She raced up to her room and scrambled up on the table. The sun was setting. The sky was brilliant with streamers of red and gold. She had the feeling she was thousands of miles away from her small, ugly room, the kitchen, the schoolroom, and Miss Minchin's scolding.

Suddenly, a head emerged from the attic window next door. It was an Indian man, a servant. He held a monkey in his arms. He had a faraway look in his eye.

He's homesick, Sara thought. She smiled at him.

He smiled back. Just then, the monkey broke loose and, chattering, ran across the roof straight into Sara's room!

"Will he let me catch him?" Sara called out in Hindustani, the man's native language.

The Indian man was surprised and delighted to hear words of his own language coming from this lovely little girl. "He's fast," he answered her, "and hard to catch. If you will permit me, I will catch him."

Sara agreed. The man steadily and lightly crossed over the roof to her room. He quickly captured the monkey.

He looked around her room and then back at Sara. He was confused. Room and girl did not match. Finally, he bowed. "Ram Dass at your service," he said.

"How do you do?" Sara said politely.

Ram Dass then crossed the roof again, as agile as the monkey, and disappeared through his window.

Sara stood in the middle of the room and thought of the many things his face and manner had brought back to her. Her life in India, with servants all around, seemed like a far-off dream. It was over. Her life had changed. This room and her work downstairs—these were her life now.

But one thing hadn't changed. She was still Sara Crewe. "Whatever happens," she said aloud, "inside, I am still Papa's Little Princess. So what if I wear rags? It's easy to be a princess in silks and gold. It's a challenge to be one when no one knows."

Sara held her head higher as she worked. And she was always kind, no matter what the others said or did. She looked forward to errands, regardless of the weather, because they gave her the chance to learn more about the old gentleman next door.

Though Ram Dass and the other servants were Indian, the owner of the house was not. He was an Englishman like her father. His name was Mr. Carrisford. He had made a great deal of money and thought it lost. Though he had regained his fortune, he had almost died of brain fever and was still ill. His troubles, like those of Sara's father, had been connected with diamond mines.

Sara wished she could make Mr. Carrisford well again and bring a smile to his sad face. When she looked out her attic window, she would wish him goodnight. Perhaps kind thoughts reached people, even through walls and doors.

Just as she was learning about Mr. Carrisford, he was learning about her. Janet and Nora, of the "Large Family," told him about the-little-girl-who-is-not-a-beggar. And Ram Dass told him about the adventure with the wandering monkey. "She lives in such a poor room," he said, "and still she smiles."

"Do you suppose," Mr. Carrisford said to Mr. Carmichael, "that Ralph Crewe's child is living in such miserable conditions?" He put his head in his hands. After a long silence, he said, "I must find her. If she is penniless, it is my fault. Poor Crewe put every penny he had into my plan. He trusted me. And he died thinking I had ruined him."

"We'll find her," Mr. Carmichael said. "It's just a matter of time."

"In the meantime," Mr. Carrisford said, "I would like to do something for the-little-girl-who-is-not-a-beggar."

One night, after running extra errands, Sara got home too late for supper. She had already missed dinner earlier that day, and she was now very hungry. She could barely climb the stairs to her room.

Ermengarde waited for her.

"You look tired, Sara," she said.

Sara nodded weakly.

"I wish I was as thin as you," Ermengarde said, not knowing how hungry her friend was.

For the first time since Ermengarde had known her, Sara broke down and cried.

A thought came to Ermengarde. Sara was hungry! "Sara," she said, "my aunt sent me a box of treats—cakes and meat pies, jam tarts and buns. I'll go get it."

Sara reeled. "Could you?" A sudden light sprang into Sara's eyes. "We'll pretend it's a party! We'll invite Becky!"

While Ermengarde sneaked back to her room, Sara got Becky. The two of them got ready for the party. Ermengarde's red shawl became the tablecloth. An old package of handkerchiefs became plates of pure gold. Artificial flowers from an old hat became roses for the center of the table.

When Ermengarde returned, the room had been transformed into a grand banquet hall.

The three little girls had just sat down to their feast when they heard someone coming up the stairs.

"Miss Minchin!" croaked Becky.

The door flew open. Miss Minchin was pale with rage. "I suspected something like this," she cried. "Lavinia was telling the truth!" She grabbed Becky. "Go to your room!" she commanded. Then she turned on Sara. "This is your idea," she said. "You get nothing to eat tomorrow." She took Ermengarde and the box of food and left the room, slamming the door behind her.

The dream was at an end. The gold plates were again nothing but handkerchiefs; the roses, old, fake flowers. Sara felt terribly weary. She sat on the edge of her bed and sobbed. She was so tired, she soon fell into a deep sleep.

Several hours later, Sara awoke feeling warm and comfortable. "I don't want to wake up," she murmured. "I feel as if I'm covered in a soft, warm blanket, and there's a fire nearby."

She opened her eyes slowly. She couldn't believe her eyes. She rubbed them and looked again. A fire glowed in the little stove. A kettle boiled on it. A new table sat next to her bed—and a desk and books. A thick carpet lay on the floor, a beautiful quilt on her bed. Best of all, a dish heaped with sandwiches and cakes was laid out on the table.

Sara leaped out of bed. "I'm still dreaming!" she exclaimed. Then she saw a note on the table. "To the little girl in the attic" it read, "from a friend."

Sara rushed to get Becky. Together they crouched by the fire and sampled the food. There was soup and sandwiches and muffins and tea.

"You see, Becky," Sara said. "It's magic! Magic won't ever let anything get too terrible."

"Oh, miss," Becky said. "It must be a dream."

"Things don't taste this good in dreams," Sara said.

The next morning, Miss Minchin couldn't believe her eyes. She expected to see a pale, defeated Sara, her eyes swollen from crying. Instead, she saw a girl with a spring in her step and color in her cheeks. "You do not seem to understand," Miss Minchin said. "You are in disgrace."

"I know that," Sara replied. She couldn't stop smiling.

Miss Minchin treated Sara more harshly than ever, but Sara worked with a light heart now. She had a secret and nothing could wipe that away.

Every night and every morning, Sara and Becky found meals laid out for them. There were other surprises: a beautiful robe, little statues, pictures, books, and more books. And always the same note appeared: "from a friend."

One day not long afterward, when Sara took in the mail,
she saw a package addressed "To the little girl in the right-
hand attic room."

Miss Munchin saw it too. "Give me that," she snapped.

"It's for me," Sara told her.

"Then open it," Miss Minchin commanded.

Inside were a dress, coat, hat, stockings, and shoes. They were made of the finest materials. A note was attached to the coat: "To be worn every day. Will be replaced when necessary."

Miss Minchin's face went white. Could she have made a mistake? Did Sara have a rich relative somewhere? "Put the clothes on and come to the classroom," she directed Sara. "Forget the rest of your errands."

When the other girls saw Sara in her fine new clothes, they were amazed. "What if she really is a...princess?" they whispered to one another.

Sara and Becky had a hearty laugh over that later as they ate their supper.

"I wish I knew who was doing all this," Sara said. She sat down to write a note. She would leave it on her table where her new friend would find it. As she signed it, there was a tapping at the window.

"The Indian gentleman's monkey!" Becky cried.

Sara ran to the window. "It's too cold for him out there," she said as she opened the window and took the monkey into her arms.

Becky was struck by a thought. "Do you suppose it's the little monkey that could be doing all these magical things?"

"I don't know," Sara said. "With magic, anything's possible."

It was too late to take the monkey back home, so Sara kept him in her warm little room. When she fell asleep, he curled up at the foot of her bed.

Early the next day, no one at the house next door seemed to miss the monkey. That was because Mr. Carmichael had just returned that morning from Paris where he had been searching for Captain Crewe's little girl. The news he brought back with him was not good. He had failed to find her.

"Perhaps we've been wrong to think she was in Paris," Mr. Carmichael said. "It is true that her mother was French. But Captain Crewe may have brought her here to England where he grew up."

Mr. Carrisford nodded. He was very sad. "We must find her," he said. "We'll search everywhere in London if need be. I don't care what it takes or how long. Start with the school next door. There is a little girl there..."

At that very moment, Mr. Carrisford was interrupted by a knock at the door. When Ram Dass opened it, Sara was smiling up at him. "I've brought back your monkey," she said.

Ram Dass brought Sara into the study. She was surprised to see the entire "Large Family" gathered around Mr. Carrisford.

"It is the little girl from next door," Ram Dass said. "I thought you might like to meet her." Then he took the monkey from Sara.

Sara thanked him in his native language.

Mr. Carrisford couldn't believe his ears. "How do you know that language, child?" he asked in surprise.

"I was born in India," she replied.

A lump rose in the old man's throat. "Question her," he directed Mr. Carmichael. "I cannot."

Mr. Carmichael led Sara to a large armchair and asked her about her old home and family. She told about her father. "He died," she said, "because he trusted a friend too much over some diamond mines."

Mr. Carrisford rose up out of his chair. "It is the child!" he cried. "She is the child!"

"What child?" Sara asked. "What child am I?"

Mr. Carmichael explained. Mr. Carrisford had been her father's friend. He had thought there were no diamonds. He was sick with brain fever when he found out he had been wrong. By that time, Captain Crewe was dead. "We've been looking for you for two years," he concluded.

"And all the time, I was on the other side of the wall," Sara said. She turned to Mr. Carrisford. "Was it you who brought the magic to my room in the attic?"

Mr. Carrisford nodded. There were tears in his eyes.

Sara ran to him and threw her arms around him. A warm glow came over Mr. Carrisford's face. For the first time in a long while, he felt he would get healthy again. And indeed he would.

Everyone was beaming with joy when suddenly there was another knock at the door. Ram Dass slipped out to open it. In the doorway was Miss Minchin, scowling. He showed her into the study.

"I heard one of my servants had come over here," said Miss Minchin, obviously annoyed. "I have come to take her back.

I can assure you she will never bother you again."

Mr. Carrisford looked at her sternly. "Sara Crewe is my late partner's little princess," he said. "She will live here with me now."

Miss Minchin's face turned red. All she could think about now was the money she'd lose if the girl didn't return. "Sara was always a good student." She turned toward Sara. "Why don't you come back to the school?" she asked. "I've always liked you, you know."

Sara looked Miss Minchin right in the eye. "Have you?" she asked. "I didn't know that."

Rejected by the little girl she had mistreated for so long, Miss Minchin turned on her heels and left the house.

In the years that followed, Miss Minchin was often seen peeking out the school windows. She watched a sight more hateful to her than anything else: Sara Crewe, dressed in the finest clothes, her eyes shining, standing on the steps to the house next door. Becky, who had also gone there to live, always followed her. Sometimes Lotte and Ermengarde were with Sara too. Miss Minchin could only watch, unable to do anything about it.

Still, whenever she met Miss Minchin on the street, Sara was always courteous and kind. After all, she knew something very important. No matter what, a princess can never lose her crown if she stays true to herself.

	DATE DUE		

F   Burnett, Frances
BUR   Hodgson
              A little princess